Dear Parent:
Your child's love of reading starts here!

Every child learns to read in a different way and at his or her own speed.
You can help your young reader improve and become more confident
by encouraging his or her own interests and abilities. You can also guide
your child's spiritual development by reading stories with biblical values
and Bible stories, like I Can Read! books published by Zonderkidz. From
books your child reads with you to the first books he or she reads alone,
there are I Can Read! books for every stage of reading:

SHARED READING
Basic language, word repetition, and whimsical
illustrations, ideal for sharing with your emergent reader.

BEGINNING READING
Short sentences, familiar words, and simple concepts for
children eager to read on their own.

READING WITH HELP
Engaging stories, longer sentences, and language play
for developing readers.

READING ALONE
Complex plots, challenging vocabulary, and high-interest
topics for the independent reader.

ADVANCED READING
Short paragraphs, chapters, and exciting themes for the
perfect bridge to chapter books.

I Can Read! books have introduced children to the joy of reading since
1957. Featuring award-winning authors and illustrations and a fabulous
cast of beloved characters, I Can Read books for
beginning readers.

A lifetime of discovery begins with the magical words "I Can Read!"

*Visit www.icanread.com for information on enriching your child's reading experience.
Visit www.zonderkidz.com for more Zonderkidz I Can Read! titles.*

Blessed are those who show mercy.
They will be shown mercy.
— Matthew 5:7 NIrV

ZONDERKIDZ

Dial 'M' for Mess Up
©2013 Big Idea Entertainment, LLC. VEGGIETALES®, character names, likenesses
and other indicia are trademarks of and copyrighted by Big Idea Entertainment, LLC.
All rights reserved.
Illustrations ©2011 by Big Idea Entertainment, Inc.

Requests for information should be addressed to:

Zonderkidz, 5300 Patterson Ave SE, Grand Rapids, Michigan 49530

ISBN 978-0-310-74167-1

Editor: Mary Hassinger
Art direction: Karen Poth
Cover design: Karen Poth
Interior design: Ron Eddy

Printed in China

14 15 16 17 18 19 /DSC/ 20 19 18 17 16 15 14 13 12 11 10 9 8 7 6 5 4 3 2

I Can Read!™

Dial 'M' for Mess Up

story by Karen Poth

My name is Detective Larry.
This is my partner, Bob.
He carries a badge.
I carry my badger.

Together we
solve mysteries.
Here is one of
our stories.

It was early in the morning.

RING!

A call came in.

It was Percy Pea.

He was in a big mess!

He needed our help.

We met Percy downtown.
"I was helping Laura
deliver newspapers,"
Percy said.

"I put her money in my pocket.

But it fell out.

She is going to be mad."

I saw Laura coming.
She didn't look mad.

"Percy," Bob said.

"Laura won't be mad.

It was an accident.

Tell her the truth."

Percy told Laura the truth.

She smiled.

"It's okay, Percy," Laura said.

"I forgive you."

This case was closed.

I wrote that in my book.

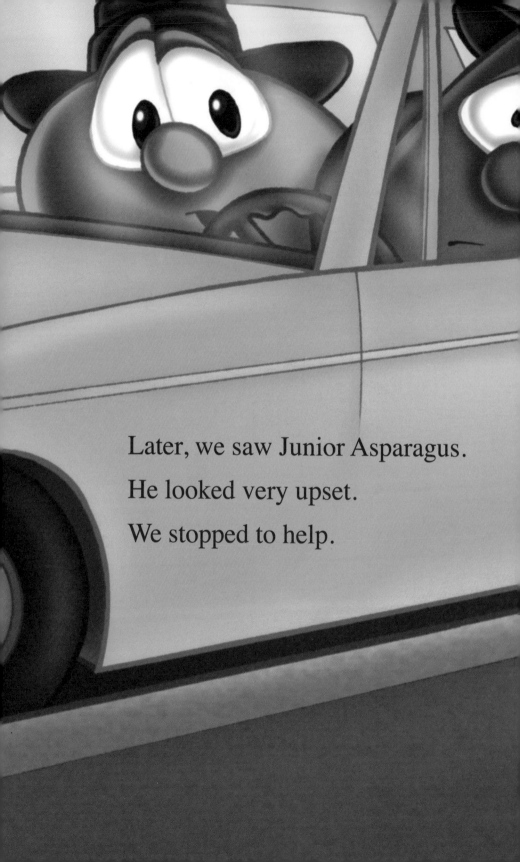

Later, we saw Junior Asparagus.

He looked very upset.

We stopped to help.

"What's wrong?" I asked.
"I was helping Percy Pea
sell lemonade," Junior said.
"I lost his money."

"I set the dollar on the table,"
said Junior.
"It blew away!

"I told Percy
and he got really mad."
Junior felt very bad.

Percy wasn't being nice!

I got back in the car.

I called Percy Pea.

He didn't answer.

Then I saw him.

Percy was running.

I drove fast.

We caught up to him.

"Stop!" Bob shouted.

"Why are you running?"

"I'm running from Laura Carrot,"
Percy said.

"She's really mad."

"Why is Laura mad?"
Bob asked.

"She changed
her mind,"
Percy said.
"She wants her
money back."

"Why did she change
her mind?"
Bob asked.

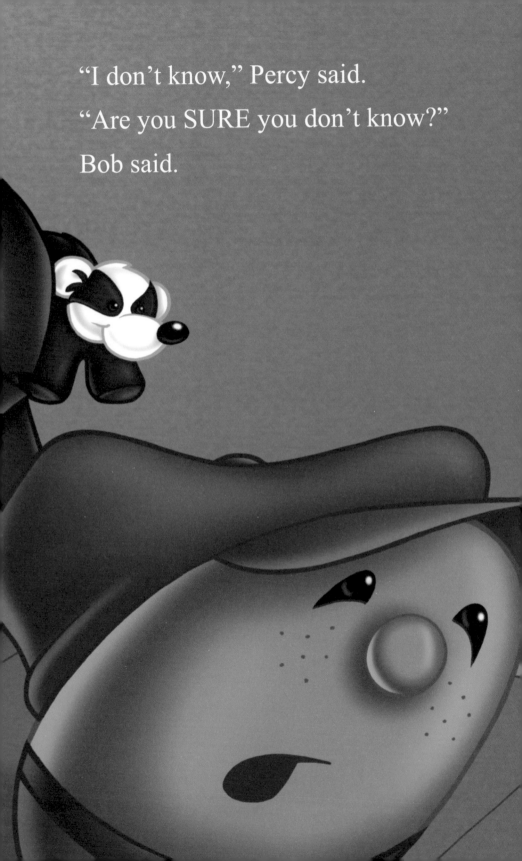

"I don't know," Percy said.

"Are you SURE you don't know?"
Bob said.

Then it happened.
"Laura's mad because
I was mean to Junior,"
Percy said.
Percy started to cry.

"It's okay," I said. "We all mess up sometimes. God wants us to forgive."

Percy looked up.
"I have to find
Junior," he said.
"I'm going to
forgive him."

Percy ran to find his friend.

Later that day Bob and I were driving in the car. We saw something that made us smile!

Percy, Junior, and Laura
were together.
They were selling
lemonade AND newspapers.